Dear Parents:

Congratulations! Your child is taking the first steps on an exciting journey. The destination? Independent reading!

STEP INTO READING® will help your child get there. The program offers five steps to reading success. Each step includes fun stories and colorful art or photographs. In addition to original fiction and books with favorite characters, there are Step into Reading Non-Fiction Readers, Phonics Readers and Boxed Sets, Sticker Readers, and Comic Readers—a complete literacy program with something to interest every child.

Learning to Read, Step by Step!

Ready to Read   Preschool–Kindergarten
• big type and easy words • rhyme and rhythm • picture clues
For children who know the alphabet and are eager to begin reading.

Reading with Help   Preschool–Grade 1
• basic vocabulary • short sentences • simple stories
For children who recognize familiar words and sound out new words with help.

Reading on Your Own   Grades 1–3
• engaging characters • easy-to-follow plots • popular topics
For children who are ready to read on their own.

Reading Paragraphs   Grades 2–3
• challenging vocabulary • short paragraphs • exciting stories
For newly independent readers who read simple sentences with confidence.

Ready for Chapters   Grades 2–4
• chapters • longer paragraphs • full-color art
For children who want to take the plunge into chapter books but still like colorful pictures.

STEP INTO READING® is designed to give every child a successful reading experience. The grade levels are only guides; children will progress through the steps at their own speed, developing confidence in their reading. The F&P Text Level on the back cover serves as another tool to help you choose the right book for your child.

Remember, a lifetime love of reading starts with a single step!

For Derek, Tracey, Heidi, and
Raymond's Random House family
—V.M.N.

For my friend Vaunda
—D.A.

Text copyright © 2022 by Vaunda Micheaux Nelson
Cover art and interior illustrations copyright © 2022 by Derek Anderson

All rights reserved. Published in the United States by Random House Children's Books, a division of Penguin Random House LLC, New York.

Step into Reading, Random House, and the Random House colophon are registered trademarks of Penguin Random House LLC.

Visit us on the Web!
rhcbooks.com

Educators and librarians, for a variety of teaching tools, visit us at RHTeachersLibrarians.com

Library of Congress Cataloging-in-Publication Data is available upon request.
ISBN 978-0-593-56371-7 (trade) — ISBN 978-0-593-56372-4 (lib. bdg.) —
ISBN 978-0-593-56373-1 (ebook)

Printed in the United States of America
10 9 8 7 6 5 4 3 2 1

This book has been officially leveled by using the F&P Text Level Gradient™ Leveling System.

READY? SET. BIRTHDAY!

✦A RAYMOND AND ROXY BOOK✦

by Vaunda Micheaux Nelson
illustrated by Derek Anderson

Random House 🏠 New York

Making Time Fly

Raymond wants
his birthday
to come fast.

"Go play," Mama says.

"Time flies
when you have fun."

Raymond bounces a ball.

He bounces it fast.

He bounces it faster.

But time does not fly.

Roxy skates by.

Raymond chases her.
He wishes he had
skates.

"Roxy, let's have fun
so time will fly."
Roxy laughs.
She lets Raymond
try her skates.
They do not fit.

Raymond watches
Roxy skate.

He is not having fun.
Time does not fly.

Scrubs and Drips

"Help me wash the car,"
Papa says.

Raymond does not want to.

He wants time to fly.

Papa gets water and rags.
Raymond and Roxy
soap up the car.

Raymond scrubs Roxy.
Roxy scrubs Raymond.

Papa sprays the car.

Papa sprays Raymond.

Papa sprays Roxy.

They run and scream.

Raymond and Roxy

spray Papa.

Papa runs and screams.

They all shine the car.

Roxy drips home.

"Can we wash the car tomorrow?" Raymond asks. "But tomorrow is your birthday," says Papa. Raymond grins.

"We had fun
and time *did* fly!"

"Sleeping makes time fly,
too," Mama says.

Raymond hops into bed.
He dreams of clocks
with wings.

The Present

"Hooray!"

It is Raymond's birthday.

He leaps out of bed.

Then he stops.
He does not want
speed today.

Raymond wants his
birthday to last.
He creeps to the kitchen
as slow as a snail.

He eats breakfast
as slow as a sloth.

"Are you sick?" Mama asks.

"No," Raymond says.

"I want today to last."

"Happy birthday!"

Mama and Papa shout.

They give him a present.

"Thanks," Raymond says.

He starts to unwrap it.

Then he stops.

"I will open it later."

"Raymond *must* be sick,"

says Papa.

Later, Roxy comes over.

"Open your present!"
she says.

"Not yet," says Raymond.

"Open it!" Roxy says.
Raymond *wants*
to open the present.
He pulls off the ribbon.

"Hurry!" says Roxy.

He pulls off the tape.

"Now!" Roxy says.

He rips off the paper.

"Skates!" Raymond shouts.

He hugs Mama and Papa.

"Come on, Roxy!"

Raymond says.

"We should sing first,"
says Mama.

Raymond blows out
his candles fast.

He eats his cake fast.
"Our Raymond is feeling
better," Papa says.

Raymond loves his gift.
Now he and Roxy
can skate fast together—
if he can keep
from falling.